Dear Parent:

Psst . . . you're looking at the Super Secret Weapon of Reading. It's called comics.

STEP INTO READING® COMIC READERS are a perfect step in learning to read. They provide visual cues to the meaning of words and helpfully break out short pieces of dialogue into speech balloons.

Here are some terms commonly associated with comics:
   PANEL: A section of a comic with a box drawn around it.
   CAPTION: Narration that helps set the scene.
   SPEECH BALLOON: A bubble containing dialogue.
   GUTTER: The space between panels.

Tips for reading comics with your child:

• Have your child read the speech balloons while you read the captions.
• Ask your child: What is a character feeling? How can you tell?
• Have your child draw a comic showing what happens after the book is finished.

STEP INTO READING® COMIC READERS are designed to engage and to provide an empowering reading experience. They are also fun. The best-kept secret of comics is that they create lifelong readers. **And that will make you the real hero of the story!**

Jennifer L. Holm and Matthew Holm
Co-creators of the Babymouse and Squish series

Published in the United States by Random House Children's Books, a division of Penguin Random House LLC, 1745 Broadway, New York, NY 10019, and in Canada by Penguin Random House Canada Limited, Toronto. Step into Reading, Random House, and the Random House colophon are registered trademarks of Penguin Random House LLC.

Visit us on the Web!
StepIntoReading.com
rhcbooks.com

Educators and librarians, for a variety of teaching tools, visit us at RHTeachersLibrarians.com

ISBN 978-0-593-18029-7 (trade) — ISBN 978-0-593-30431-0 (lib. bdg.) — ISBN 978-0-593-30432-7 (ebook)

Printed in the United States of America   10 9 8 7 6 5 4 3 2 1

STEP 3 INTO READING®

STEP 3 READING ON YOUR OWN

A COMIC READER

JURASSIC WORLD
CAMP CRETACEOUS

LOST IN THE WILD!

adapted by Steve Behling
illustrated by Patrick Spaziante

Random House 🏠 New York

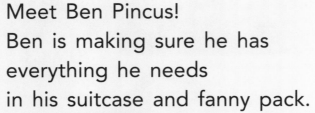

Meet Ben Pincus!
Ben is making sure he has
everything he needs
in his suitcase and fanny pack.

Do I have enough
hand sanitizer?

Ben is nervous.
He doesn't like
being away from home.

He's going to a camp.
But it's not just *any* camp.

Ben is going to Camp Cretaceous!
It's at Jurassic World.
It may be the coolest camp ever!
He will be on an island . . .
with dinosaurs!

Ben meets the other campers.
Everyone is excited
to see dinosaurs!
Well, everyone but Ben.

Camp is off to a good start.
Everyone is having a great time!
Well, everyone but Ben.

Then something happens.
The dinosaurs run wild!
The dinosaurs rampage!

The campers are stranded
by themselves.
They must find a way
off the island.

Run for
the monorail!

Then Ben realizes he doesn't have his fanny pack anymore. No fanny pack means no hand sanitizer!

No map.
No snacks.
Only germs.

Ben is getting hungry. He and Bumpy find a bush with big red berries.

Bumpy dives right in and eats a whole bunch. But Ben doesn't like the taste.

Yuck!

CHOMP!

Ben and Bumpy run away from the Stegosaurus. They find a valley.

I see something, Bumpy!

It's a road!
Ben knows that all roads lead to the Main Park.
If they go there, they can turn on an emergency beacon!

Toro sees Ben.
He starts running after him!
Ben heads for the trees.

Ben and Bumpy get away!
But with Toro guarding
his territory, they will not
be able to get past.

Ben looks around his campsite.
He sees Bumpy's footprint.
If only he hadn't been
so mean to his friend.

Who's that?

Ben hears a noise and looks up.
There are glowing eyes
watching him.
He is super scared!

Ben trips on a log
and falls into a puddle of mud.
The Compys come closer . . .
and closer!

Ben closes his eyes.
Suddenly, he feels a strength
he has never felt before.
He stands up
and screams at the Compys!

Ben learns to survive on his own.
He eats bugs and berries,
and he's not afraid
of germs anymore.
He climbs trees to avoid Toro.

One day, Ben decides he is done letting Toro keep him from Main Street.
Bumpy returns to join Ben.
She is much bigger now!

Ben is glad to have his pal back.
They face Toro together.
Ben is ready this time.
He isn't going to run away.

RRRROAR!

Toro runs at Ben and Bumpy.
But Ben isn't scared!
He stands his ground.

ARRRRRGGGHHH!